The Secret Rescuers

The BABY FIREBIRD

Paula Harrison

illustrated by SOPHY WILLIAMS

nosy crow

 For Martha,
my awesome niece

First published in the UK in 2016 by Nosy Crow Ltd
The Crow's Nest, 10a Lant St
London, SE1 1QR, UK

Nosy Crow and associated logos are trademarks and/or
registered trademarks of Nosy Crow Ltd

Text copyright © Paula Harrison, 2016
Illustrations © Sophy Williams, 2016

Printed and bound in the UK by Clays Ltd, St Ives Plc

Papers used by Nosy Crow are made from wood grown in sustainable forests.

ISBN: 978 0 85763 608 9

www.nosycrow.com

Chapter One
The Enchanted Stone

Talia squashed a ball of red-brown clay between her hands. She was sitting on the wooden step at the front of her house. Her bright-green dress was smeared with clay and her bare feet were dusty. A row of freshly made cups and plates were drying in the sun beside her.

She squeezed the clay harder. She was going to make a beautiful bowl and later, when it was dry, she'd decorate it. Maybe she'd paint red Izzala flowers on the side. The prettiest bowls always sold well at the market.

1

She bent her head as she moulded the bowl into shape. Her long dark-brown hair fell over her shoulders. The sun beat down and the clay felt warm between her fingers.

In the distance, Talia could hear the sounds of the rainforest. She loved to listen to the calls of the parrots and the scratching of the grasshoppers. Many of the pictures she chose for her pottery came from the plants and animals she'd seen in the forest.

Kura, the village where Talia lived, was in the middle of the Hundred Valleys at the southernmost tip of the Kingdom of Arramia. The little valleys lay side by side, divided by tall mountains and filled with tropical rainforest. Among them was the most secret place of all – the valley of Jalmar, where the magical firebirds lived.

Many enchanted creatures lived in the Kingdom of Arramia. There were dragons, sky unicorns and star wolves, but many of them lived far away in the north of the country. The firebirds' valley lay just across the river. Talia often ran down to the water to watch them glide from tree to tree on the opposite bank.

Tiny golden flames sparkled on their wings.

Talia knew the flames must be magical, as they never scorched the flowers or leaves. She longed to get closer to the amazing birds but she knew she mustn't cross the river. Entering the hidden valley was forbidden. That was the law of her village and Talia knew the rule had been made to keep the firebirds safe!

Smoothing the rim of the bowl, Talia held it up to check it looked good all the way round. She placed it next to the other things she'd made and brushed the clay off her hands. Her mind drifted as she gazed at the swaying treetops in the distance. Something so strange and so amazing had happened last week that she could hardly stop thinking about it!

She'd been walking in the rainforest, gathering berries that she could use to make different-coloured paints. A rising wind had rocked the trees and a dragon had swooped through the air, landing in a clearing up ahead. Talia had nearly dropped all her berries when she saw a girl with blonde plaits slip down from the dragon's back.

Sophy, the dragon-riding girl, had said she'd flown all the way from the royal castle where she worked as a maid. Then she'd given Talia a very special gift – a stone that magically broke open and had sparkling orange crystals inside. It was so beautiful! Talia could hardly believe it was hers.

She put her hand to her neck. Yes, the stone was still safe. She'd tied it on to some thread so that she could wear it as a necklace. It hung beneath her dress where no one could see. The girl on the dragon had told her to keep it a secret. She'd told Talia something else too. Something amazing.

She'd said the stone would let her talk to magical animals.

Talia took out the tiny rock. Her mum had gone to water the vegetables so she was quite alone. Gently opening the stone, she gazed

at the little hollow filled with orange crystals. They glittered so brightly they made Talia think of flames.

Could it be true? Could this stone really let her speak to magical creatures?

Sophy had called it a Speaking Stone. She'd also explained that magical animals were in danger from people who wanted to capture them. It had all begun with Sir Fitzroy, a horrible knight who hated the creatures. Talia had listened carefully. She really wanted to help.

Every day since then, Talia had wandered in the rainforest trying to find a magical animal to see if the girl's promise about the stone was really true. She'd searched and searched, but she hadn't found a single creature and her mum had told her off for not finishing her chores!

Talia hung the stone around her neck again and began putting on her sandals. The pottery would be dry in two hours. She had enough time for a walk in the forest. As she fastened her buckle, there was a faint rustling noise.

Talia looked up. Had she imagined it or
was something hiding in that bush? The plant
rustled again. This time Talia saw the branches
move. She crept forwards, expecting to see
an emerald lizard or a brown piper bird.
A golden head poked out between the leaves.
The creature had a dark beak and two bright
eyes. A sparkle of flame flickered on its head.

Talia stifled a gasp. It was a firebird –
probably a young one because it was quite
small.

Firebirds *never* came into the village! They
were shy creatures and hardly ever ventured out
of their hidden valley. This one was a long way
from home. Maybe it was lost?

Crouching down, Talia gently held out her
hand. She knew the flames sparkling among a
firebird's feathers wouldn't hurt her. Every tale
she'd ever listened to told her that! "Hello, I'm
Talia," she said softly. "Are you lost?"

The firebird gave a startled squawk and drew
its head back into the bush.

"Don't worry! I won't hurt you!" Talia tiptoed
closer. Peering into the bush, she found the bird
gazing back at her. A breathless excitement
gripped her. If the Speaking Stone was working,
then this firebird would understand what she
was saying!

She tried again. "Hello, I'm Talia!"

"Riki!" cheeped the bird, sticking out its beak.

"Sorry?" Talia wasn't sure she'd heard right.

"Riki!" The firebird crept out of the bush and peered up at her. "That's my name!"

"Wow! You understood me!" Talia's stomach flipped over. "Then it's true. The stone really *does* work!"

"What stone?" Riki tilted his head to one side.

"I have a special stone that lets me talk to you – see!" Talia pulled out her Speaking Stone and opened it to show him the crystals inside.

Riki flapped his wings in excitement. Tiny flickers of flame glittered among his golden feathers. "I love it!" he squawked. "It's so pretty!"

"You're a long way from your valley," Talia told him. "Are you lost?"

Riki shook his head. "I wanted to see everything! My family told me about your wooden houses with the funny see-through squares."

"You mean windows," said Talia, smiling.

"Yes, windows!" Riki flapped his wings again. "It sounded so amazing. I just had to see! They said I was too little and it wasn't safe, but I came anyway!"

"You're very brave," Talia told him. "But are you sure your family won't be worried about you?"

A faint cough came from nearby.

"What's that noise?" Riki lifted his beak as if he was sniffing the air. "There's another human over there. I think it's a boy."

"Where?" Talia twisted round in alarm. A boy was peeking round the corner of the next house. Talia recognised his cheeky face and untidy black hair. "Lucas! What are you doing?"

Lucas came out, looking sheepish. "There's a game of Twist Ball starting. I came to see if you wanted to play. Then I saw you with that bird." His eyes darted to Riki. "Why are you talking as if you know what it's saying?"

Talia's heart sank. She and Lucas were friends but she hadn't planned to tell him about the Speaking Stone. It was supposed to be a secret! What was she going to do now?

Chapter Two
The Riders from Far Away

Talia sprang up, facing Lucas. Her fingers closed around the magical stone. "You shouldn't be spying on people!"

"I didn't mean to!" Lucas flushed. "I just wondered what you were doing."

Riki darted behind Talia, pressing his warm feathers against her legs. "Is the boy dangerous, Talia?"

"No, he's not dangerous," replied Talia. "Don't worry!" She saw a puzzled look on Lucas's face and she quickly decided what to do.

He was a friend. She would trust him.

"You're talking to the bird again!" said Lucas. "It can't understand you."

"Actually it can!" Talia showed him the Speaking Stone. She told him how she'd met a girl called Sophy when she was walking in the rainforest one day. She explained that Sophy had given her this stone and that now she could speak to magical animals.

"It's a special stone," she finished. "Sophy had a whole bag of them and each one only works for one person."

"Are you trying to trick me?" Lucas frowned. "You can't *really* speak to this firebird at all, can you?"

"No, it's true!" Talia didn't want Riki to hear her and get scared, so she leaned closer to whisper in Lucas's ear. "The girl who gave me the stone told me that magical animals are in danger. There are people who want to capture them. She asked me to help."

"OK, that's definitely not true!" Lucas folded his arms. "I've never met anyone who wanted to capture a magical animal."

Just then a faint drumming began in the distance. It grew louder and louder. Riki leapt into Talia's arms in fright as four riders broke through the edge of the rainforest. A pudgy man rode at the front wearing a velvet cloak and hat. The others wore grey soldiers' uniforms. They galloped up the track to the village, the dust flying beneath the horses' hooves.

Talia ducked down behind a bush, clutching Riki in her arms.

His golden feathers felt soft as he nestled against her neck. The man in the cloak glanced their way before riding on into the middle of the village.

"That's weird!" whispered Lucas. "We haven't had visitors for months."

Talia made sure the riders were gone before getting to her feet. "I wonder why they've come. I have a really bad feeling about this."

"What's wrong?" Riki's eyes widened.

Talia wondered how much to tell him. "Maybe it's nothing, but I just think we should go inside." Carrying him gently, she climbed the porch steps.

"I'll go and see who they are!" Lucas dashed down the path.

"Lucas!" Talia called after him. "Don't tell anyone about the firebird or my stone."

"I won't!" Lucas disappeared around the corner.

Once inside, Riki flew down from Talia's

arms and began exploring. He pecked at the
saucepans in the kitchen, hopped on to the
kitchen table and flapped right up to the ceiling.
Then he discovered the mirror in Talia's room
and preened in front of it for ages, admiring his
feathers.

Talia stood nervously at the window. She'd
never seen riders enter the village in such a
hurry before.

Lucas came tearing back round the corner a
few minutes later and bounded up the steps. "I
believe you now!" he panted. "I don't like those
men at all. The leader's called Lord Fortescue.
They're looking for magical creatures and they
want to search the village. We have to get that
firebird out of here!"

Talia knelt down next to Riki. "I'm taking you
back to the forest. It's not safe here any more."

Riki was still admiring himself in the mirror.
Each time he stretched his wings, flames
glittered among his feathers.

Talia heard men's voices. She peeked round the curtain and saw the soldiers approaching. Where could she hide Riki? She noticed an empty clay pot she'd made weeks ago. It was a large and had a neat round lid. It was perfect!

"Riki! I need you to hide in here." She lifted the lid to the pot. "It won't be for long, I promise!"

Riki stopped preening, surprised at her urgent tone. He peered into the pot and his beak wobbled. "But it's dark!"

"I know but I'll be holding it the whole time. Please, Riki!" said Talia. "Just get in and I'll take you back to Jalmar Valley, where you'll be safe."

"All right, Talia!" Riki fluttered his wings and jumped in.

Talia's heart ached to see him huddled inside, his wings all squashed. His little face looked up at her as she placed the lid back on, leaving a small gap so he could breathe. She lifted the heavy pot and followed Lucas down the steps.

Two men in grey uniforms were knocking at the house next door. Behind them was the pudgy man with the velvet cloak. Talia sped up. The edge of the village was not far down the track. If only they could get away without being noticed.

"Stop at once!" The plump man marched towards them. He glanced suspiciously from Lucas to Talia. "Where are you going?"

Talia's mouth went dry. What should they say? She couldn't think of a single thing.

"We're fetching water from the river." Lucas pointed to Talia's pot. "It'll take both of us to carry this home once it's full."

Talia nodded. "It gets really heavy." She hoped desperately that Riki wouldn't make a sound. She stared back at the man, noticing his flabby cheeks and the pimples on his chin with hairs sticking out of them.

The man turned away, mopping his sweaty face with a grey handkerchief. "Well, hurry up then!"

Talia and Lucas hurried down the track as fast as they dared. Talia could hear the man muttering about stupid villagers.

"That's Lord Fortescue!" hissed Lucas.

"He's the rudest and most horrid person I've ever met," cried Talia. "I wish he'd never come here!"

As they dashed into the rainforest, Talia caught the honey-sweet scent of Izzala flowers. Parrots squawked in the treetops and a hummingbird darted by in search of nectar. The huge leaves over their heads glistened with water drops from the last shower of rain.

Mist swirled around the treetops and rich brown earth crumbled under their feet.

Talia smiled in relief as the leaves closed around them, blocking their view of the village. She took the lid off the pot. "Are you all right, Riki? I'm so sorry you had to go in there!"

The little firebird popped his head out of the pot and shook it vigorously. "Can I come out now? I'm squished!"

"Yes, it's all safe!" Talia set the pot down to let Riki fly out. "We'll take you back to the river so you can find your way home."

"It's this way!" Riki soared into the treetops and fluttered from branch to branch. "Follow me!"

Talia tucked the pot under a bush where she could find it later. Then she dashed after Riki.

Lucas followed her, grumbling. "If he goes that fast we'll lose him completely."

They managed to keep track of the little firebird. Talia found it tricky dodging bushes

and branches while checking where Riki was
going. Lucas tripped over a vine and got very
muddy.

At last they came to the edge of a wide river.
The water gurgled and foamed as it poured over
the slippery rocks. This was the Amarangi
River and on the other side lay Jalmar Valley,
where the firebirds lived.

"Here we are – nearly home!" Riki flew down to Talia's shoulders. His wings felt warm against her cheek.

On the opposite bank, the twisted branches of the Izzala trees were covered with red flowers. The air smelled sweet and the glow of magic hung in the air.

Talia smiled. This was her favourite place.

It was the closest she was allowed to get to the firebirds' hidden valley. The old stories said that the place was full of Izzala trees and their branches were the only ones that a firebird would choose for building a nest.

Talia longed to visit the valley and see for herself. Sometimes she imagined she was there, walking among the trees while firebirds glided all around her. It would be like a dream come true!

Chapter Three
A Magical Message

As Talia gazed across the foamy river at the
firebirds' valley, she saw a bird with golden
feathers hopping along the bank. The bird was
much larger than Riki and the bright crest on its
head gleamed in the sunlight.

Riki flapped his wings excitedly. "Come with
me, Talia! Come and see Jalmar Valley."

"I'd love to, but I can't," sighed Talia. "Jalmar
belongs to you. The law of my village says that
we have to leave you in peace. You shouldn't
come back to our village either. It's not safe

there any more!"

Riki's tail feathers drooped. "But you can come here to the river and visit me!"

"I'll come as soon as I can," promised Talia. Seeing Lucas's puzzled face, she remembered that her friend couldn't understand the firebird. "Riki says we should come and see him again."

"Sure!" Lucas stared at a puff of smoke rising from the opposite valley. "What's that? Have the other birds set fire to something?"

"Of course not! We firebirds do not burn things," said Riki, shaking his beak. "That is the sleeping breath of the red-back dragon. Goodbye, Talia! Goodbye, boy!" He leapt into the air and soared across the river, flames sparkling on his wings.

"Riki just said the smoke is the breath of a sleeping dragon." Talia felt excitement flutter inside her.

"Really?" Lucas's eyes widened. "I didn't know that Jalmar valley had a dragon!"

Talia found the pot and filled it with water just in case she met Lord Fortescue again on their return. When they got back to Kura, she and Lucas found everyone gathered in the middle of the village. Lord Fortescue was at the centre of the throng, surrounded by his men. He'd climbed on to a wooden box and was pointing his plump finger at the crowd.

"Don't tell me that you don't know. I think you do!" he yelled. "I will ask you one more time. WHERE do the firebirds live and where is this Cave of Wonders?"

The crowd was silent. Some people shook their heads. Others were staring at the ground. Talia's heart sank. The Cave of Wonders was meant to be an amazing underground place somewhere in the hidden valley. No one knew if it was real but it was mentioned in lots of the old stories.

"You!" Lord Fortescue shouted, pointing straight at Talia. "What do you know about this

Cave of Wonders?"

Talia felt like his finger was pinning her to the spot, but she knew she had to be brave. "I don't know anything," she told him. "It's probably just a story." She met his angry gaze. It was the truth. No one knew anything for certain because no one had ever seen the cave.

"With a name like that, it's probably full of treasure," said one of the soldiers. "That's why they don't want to tell us where it is. They want all the gold for themselves."

Lord Fortescue rubbed his chubby hands together. "This is good! We'll capture the dratted birds AND get ourselves some treasure." He addressed the crowd again. "By order of the queen I shall imprison these firebirds. As magical creatures, they are a danger to Her Majesty and to all people in the kingdom." He unrolled a parchment and showed them the queen's seal of approval. "If anyone here tries to stop us, I'll have them locked up too."

"I can't believe the queen agreed to all this," Lucas whispered to Talia. "It makes no sense!"

"But it's exactly what Sophy told me," murmured Talia. "She's a maid at the royal castle. She said there's a bad knight called Sir Fitzroy who persuaded the queen that all magical animals are dangerous."

The crowd began to scatter, and Talia and Lucas hurried away.

"So what do we do now?" said Lucas. "In the morning, Lord Sweaty-pants will go into the forest and try to find the hidden valley."

"Sophy said if there was trouble I could send a golden songbird to fetch her," explained Talia. "I have to find one right now."

"But how will she come all that way?" Lucas looked doubtful. "The queen's castle is miles from here."

Talia grinned. "She'll fly here on a dragon. That's how she came here before!"

It didn't take long for Talia to find a golden songbird. They flew past the village quite often. Now that she had her magical stone, all she had to do was call for one. She gave the little golden bird her message for Sophy and went to sleep that night feeling glad that help would come the next day.

Talia woke early in the morning and hurried to the edge of the village. She wanted to meet Sophy as soon as she landed and explain how dangerous Lord Fortescue was. They had to be careful.

But instead of a dragon with enormous green wings, the same golden songbird fluttered down to perch on her hand.

"Dear Talia, I have a message for you," sang the little bird. "Sophy is so sorry, but she cannot come to help you. There is danger at the castle and Sir Fitzroy is watching everyone closely. If she gets a chance, she will come another day."

"But the soldiers will search for the firebirds today!" cried Talia.

"I'm sorry not to bring better news," trilled the songbird before flying away.

Talia bit her thumbnail. If Sophy couldn't help she would have to try to protect the firebirds herself. She would start by finding the soldiers and following them into the rainforest.

An hour later she was watching Lord Fortescue and his men pack up their things. Her mum had gone to the market to sell the pottery and wouldn't be back till late. Talia was watching the soldiers so closely she didn't notice Lucas creeping up behind her. She jumped when he tapped her on the shoulder.

"What's happening?" whispered Lucas.

"They're getting ready to leave," Talia told him. "I've decided to follow them. I have to stop them getting too close to the hidden valley."

"What about your friend with the dragon?"

Talia sighed. "She's stuck at the castle."

"That's a shame!" Lucas grinned. "A fire-breathing dragon would be handy for chasing

Lord Fortescue!"

"Lucas!" Talia gave him a stern look.

"I'm joking!" He rolled his eyes. "I only want to scare him a bit. Anyway, if the dragon girl can't come, maybe someone else can help."

"Really? Who's that?"

"Me!" said Lucas. "I don't want those soldiers finding the hidden valley either."

"But won't your parents worry about you?"

"No, they're busy fixing our roof." Lucas folded his arms. "Don't you think tracking those men will be easier with two of us?"

Talia smiled. "It'll be *much* easier. But I don't want to get the whole village into trouble so it has to be a secret!"

Chapter Four
Tracking Lord Fortescue

Leaving their horses behind, Lord Fortescue and his soldiers set off into the rainforest. Talia and Lucas sneaked behind them, keeping their eyes on the men through the thickly growing trees.

The men stopped at a fork in the path and peered at a very old-looking map.

"Which way should we go, my lord?" The soldier pointed at the map. "I believe we're here and this is the mountain called Tam."

As if in answer, there was a deep rumble from the mountain and the ground trembled a little.

Lord Fortescue clutched
the soldier's arm till the
rumbling stopped. Then
he let go and marched up
to the fork in the path as if
he hadn't been scared at all.

Hidden behind a broad tree
trunk, Talia and Lucas watched
the men. The two children
were used to the noises of the
mountains. The firebirds' hidden
valley lay between three mountains
called Kel, Dem and Tam, and
each of them rumbled from
time to time. The old stories
said that the mountains used

to be giants. They had been turned to stone by a spell, so the tale went, but sometimes you could still hear their deep, rumbling voices.

"It's this way. I'm sure of it!" Lord Fortescue took the left-hand path and his men followed.

"They're taking the path to Tiller's Ridge and the waterfall," Lucas said into Talia's ear. "This is great! They're going completely the wrong way."

"I hope they get lost and give up on finding the valley," murmured Talia.

The men struggled on through the thick forest. Their heavy backpacks kept getting caught by low branches. They stopped more and more often to rest and drink water. Each time a parrot squawked or a wasp buzzed, they jumped. The ground sloped upwards and their steps grew slower.

By lunchtime their faces were
grim and they sat down to rest,
mopping their sweaty foreheads.

Talia and Lucas found a hiding
place behind a yellow-flowered sun bush. From
here they could see the river winding through
the forest. A thick bank of trees hid the secret
valley where the firebirds lived.

The soldier with the map unfolded the paper
and turned it round several times. Talia could
see he was looking at it upside down. "I can't
make out where we are, my lord," he said at last.
"Maybe we should go back to the village and
strike out in another direction tomorrow."

"Go back!" shouted Lord Fortescue, startling
a blue parrot in the tree above. "Don't talk such
rubbish! We shall search here the whole day and
every day until we find these firebirds!"

Talia froze. A tiny golden shape glided
through the air and disappeared behind the
bank of trees that hid the firebirds' valley from

view. She stared at the spot but the firebird had gone.

"Did you see that?" said a soldier. "There was a bright golden thing flying through the air."

"Where?" demanded Lord Fortescue. "Tell me quickly, man! You must lead us there immediately."

Talia and Lucas fled down the path as the soldiers marched back the way they'd come. They hid among the trees as the men took the track that led to the riverbank opposite Jalmar Valley.

Something fluttered in the leaves above their heads. "Talia! And the boy!" squawked Riki. "I'm so glad to see you!"

"Riki!" gasped Talia. "Shh, don't make a sound!"

As soon as the soldiers had marched on, Riki flew down to perch on Talia's shoulder. His wing brushed her cheek. She'd forgotten how warm he felt.

"Riki, why are you away from your home again?" said Talia. "It's dangerous out here!"

"Don't be cross, Talia!" Riki begged her. "I was looking for you and the boy!"

Talia hugged him. "Maybe it's a good thing you came. It's our turn to need your help! Those men are heading towards the river and if they cross the water they'll discover your valley. We have to think of a way to stop them!"

"Perhaps they'll decide there's no way to get across," said Lucas hopefully.

They sneaked further down the path to listen to the soldiers. Lord Fortescue was standing on the edge of the river pointing to the other side. No firebirds could be seen on the opposite bank,

but there was something unmistakably different
about the place. The trees were taller, the
flowers brighter and the air glittered with magic.

"This *must* be the right place," decided Lord
Fortescue.

"But, my lord, the water is too deep and the
current is moving so fast. It can't be safe to
swim," said a soldier.

"Then run back to that village and get a
boat," snapped Lord Fortescue. "One of the
villagers must have one. I shall await you here."

"What shall we do?" whispered Talia, once
they'd crept to a safe distance.

"Let's tell Lord Fortescue that we know where
the firebirds are and then take him in the wrong
direction," suggested Lucas.

Talia frowned. "What if he doesn't believe
us? I think we should warn the firebirds. They
should know how much danger they're in."

Riki fluffed his feathers and asked grumpily,
"What did the boy say? It's very tail-tickling only

to understand half of what's going on."

"Sorry, Riki," said Talia. "I wouldn't like it either."

"What did the bird say?" asked Lucas. "It's really annoying to only get part of what's happening."

Talia rolled her eyes. This was pretty annoying for her too! "Riki, we need to get across the river to Jalmar Valley before those men do. Can you help us?"

"But what about the law?" cried Lucas.

"There's a place where the water is shallow," Riki told her. "You can cross there – easy! I will show you."

"Good!" Talia turned to Lucas. "I know we're not supposed to go to the valley but someone has to talk to the firebirds. They have no idea these men are coming to capture them. But if you don't want to break the rules you should stay here."

"No way!" Lucas folded his arms. "I'm

coming too."

"This way!" Riki swooped low through the branches. "I will take you to the valley of firebird magic."

Chapter Five
The Cave of Wonders

Riki led Talia and Lucas along the riverbank.
Black clouds swarmed across the sky, and the
rain poured down. Spotting an umbrella tree,
Talia picked an enormous leaf and used it to
keep the raindrops off her head.

Riki huddled against her neck, shivering. "I
do not like the cloud water."

Talia smiled. "But the rain's good for the trees
and plants."

Riki shuddered. "The biggest Izzala tree has a
space inside its trunk. That's where I go to stay

dry when the
rain comes."

The rain shower
finished and Riki told
them to stop at a bend
in the river. The water
flowed more gently here and
instead of sharp boulders there
were smooth stepping stones.

"This way!" Riki swooped low
across the water, whistling in delight.

Lucas leapt across as fast as he could
while Talia jumped carefully from stone
to stone. When she reached the other
side, her stomach turned a
somersault. She was in the
hidden valley – the home
of the firebirds!

She gazed up at the
gigantic Izzala trees covered with beautiful red
flowers. Their honey-sweet scent filled the air.

Water drops from the rain shower glistened on every leaf and petal. Talia noticed that everything here looked bigger and brighter. Even the air she breathed seemed fresher.

Her heart leapt as she heard firebirds calling close by. "Will the other firebirds be pleased to see us?" she asked Riki. "They won't mind us being here?"

"They will love to see you!" cried Riki.

"We'd better hurry!" urged Lucas. "Those men might already have found a boat."

Talia and Lucas followed Riki over a small hill. There were no paths so they had to squeeze through the undergrowth before climbing over some rocks. They skirted round a massive hole that looked dark and deep.

"Isn't it weird that we're the first people EVER to come here?" said Lucas. "Wow, look at that huge hole!"

A column of white smoke burst from the chasm and shot into the air with a deafening hiss. Talia leapt back and grabbed hold of a tree trunk. Lucas wobbled beside the hole, trying to keep his balance.

Talia pulled him backwards and they both collapsed on the ground. The smoke stopped as suddenly as it had started.

"That was weird!" Lucas crept forwards and peered into the darkness. "I wonder what happened."

"It must be the breath of the red-back dragon," said Talia, remembering what Riki had told her.

Riki flew down. "Yes, that's the dragon's home. No point in visiting him. He's nearly always sleeping. Come on, we're almost there!"

Talia gazed curiously down the shadowy hole.

A muffled rumbling came from deep inside, like a gigantic cat purring. She wondered for a moment what the red-back dragon looked like and whether he was friendly. Riki certainly didn't seem to want to disturb the creature.

As they went deeper into the valley, Talia spotted flashes of golden wings in the trees and heard firebirds calling to each other. She strained to make out their words. "To the circle . . . to the circle of trees!"

"Come, Talia! Come, boy!" called Riki. "This is the place."

"You should call him Lucas," corrected Talia.

"Lu-cas!" squawked Riki. "I like that name."

Lucas and Talia broke through the undergrowth and found themselves in a clearing ringed by tall Izzala trees. Among the red-flowered branches were dozens of tidy nests. A flock of firebirds swooped to the ground. Many more perched in the trees, their dark eyes fixed on the children.

Talia swallowed. What if they didn't want humans in their valley? But she *had* to tell them about Lord Fortescue. "Dear firebirds!" she began, trying to speak loudly so they could all hear her. "I'm sorry to disturb you but it's an emergency!"

Before she could say more, the firebirds broke into a great chorus of squawks and cries. Lucas's eyes grew round in alarm.

"Show them your magical stone, Talia," hissed Riki.

"Oh! Yes of course!" Talia pulled the thread over her head and opened the stone to reveal the golden-orange crystals inside. "Sorry, I should have explained. I can talk to you because of this magical Speaking Stone. But there's not much time! Some bad men are trying to find your valley. They've already reached the river and when they get here you'll be in terrible danger."

One of the taller firebirds hopped forwards.

"My name is Amber-wing," she said. "We have seen these men you speak of and we have heard about the danger spreading through this kingdom. But what should we do? We are peaceful birds. We are not fighters." She spread her wings in a kind of shrug. Flames sparkled among her feathers.

"Then fly away!" cried Talia. "Go far away from this valley until the soldiers have left."

A murmur rippled through the flock of birds.

Amber-wing's beak dropped for a moment as if she was thinking. Then she shook her head. "I'm afraid we cannot leave Jalmar Valley. This is a special place for us."

Talia's heart sank. "But Lord Fortescue wants to capture you all! Please fly away – at least for a little while."

Lucas was listening hard to Talia's side of the conversation. "Why won't they leave?" he asked. "Don't they understand the danger?"

"I've tried to explain—" began Talia.

"We are the ones who should explain," interrupted Amber-wing. "You have done a brave thing coming here. We will show you why we cannot leave our valley. Come!" She flew into the air.

"They're showing us something," Talia told Lucas.

Amber-wing took them to the bottom of the rocky slope of Mount Kel. She perched next to a narrow hole in the rock. The other firebirds gathered nearby and waited for Lucas and Talia to climb through the undergrowth.

"I would like to show you the Cave of Wonders," Amber-wing said quietly.

"The Cave of Wonders!" Talia felt a shiver of excitement run down her back.

"Can I come too?" squawked Riki, hopping from foot to foot.

"Yes you may, young one." Amber-wing slipped through the crack in the rock.

Talia had to turn sideways to fit through

the narrow gap. The warmth inside washed over her like a wave. She followed the firebirds down a low tunnel, her sandals crunching on loose stones. Lucas squeezed through the thin entrance and followed her.

The dark tunnel grew brighter with every step. Talia's heart raced as she saw orange light dancing on the tunnel walls and she wondered where it came from.

At last they turned a corner and the tunnel opened into a large cavern where the floor gleamed like gold. It took Talia a moment to realise that she was actually looking at a pool of golden water. A gentle heat rose from its surface.

Riki spread his wings to bask in the warmth. "Welcome to our Cave of Wonders!"

Chapter Six
A Special Hiding Place

Talia gazed into the shining pool. The orange-gold water swirled and wisps of steam curled into the air. Her stomach flipped over.

"This is our magical fire pool," said Riki proudly.

"It's so beautiful!" breathed Talia.

"So this is what the Cave of Wonders is about," said Lucas. "Lord Fortescue was so wrong when he thought it would be full of treasure!"

"This place is special to us because it's where

our magic comes from," explained Amber-wing. "Without this fire pool we could not survive. This is why we cannot leave the valley." She sprang gracefully into the pool.

Riki squawked and jumped in too. He flapped his wings, letting the golden water run over his feathers. "I love bathing in here. It makes your wings tingle!"

"Is it lava? Like a volcano?" Talia crouched down by the pool's edge.

"No, this is a fire pool – the only one in the kingdom," said Amber-wing. "You may touch the water if you wish – it will not hurt you – but I cannot let you bathe like we do."

Talia told Lucas what the firebirds had said and how their magic came from the pool. She touched the golden surface with her finger and drew back her hand immediately, surprised by the tickly feeling in her finger. She smiled. "It feels just as magical as it looks."

"It's really warm too!" Lucas held his palms

above the pool.

Talia glanced up at the cave ceiling, that reflected the rippling golden water. Amber-wing flew out of the pool to perch on the side. Her crest gleamed and she glowed brighter than ever. The magic of the fire pool seemed to have soaked into her feathers.

"Amber-wing!" Another firebird glided down the tunnel. "The soldiers are moving! They have found a boat to cross the river."

Talia leapt up. "They're coming! We've run out of time!"

"Everyone shall hide," decided Amber-wing. "There are many places in this valley where we can stay out of sight."

The firebirds flew up the tunnel. Talia and Lucas raced after them. When they climbed back through the narrow hole, firebirds were flying everywhere and covering their nests with leaves. They hid themselves in the treetops, in rock crevices and in thick bushes.

"What about
us?" said Lucas. "If Lord
Fortescue sees us here he'll be
furious."

"We need to find somewhere to
go," agreed Talia. "Amber-wing?"
But the firebird was busy helping a
clutch of young chicks to camouflage
themselves with Izzala flowers.

"Come with me!" Riki flew
past. "I'm going to hide inside my
favourite tree."

"Will it be big enough for us?"
called Talia, but Riki had flown on.
The young firebird landed in the circle
of trees. He waved his wing towards
the tallest Izzala tree. "This is my tree!

I hide here when it rains." He ran into a gap between the jutting-out roots and suddenly disappeared.

"Riki?" Talia hurried after him. Leaning on the gnarled tree, she bent down to find an opening in the trunk that was hidden by a low branch.

"In here!" Riki's voice echoed inside the tree.

Talia bent down and crawled inside, then straightened up again. The hollow space stretched far above her head, like a very tall, thin room.

Lucas squeezed through after her. "Wow! This *is* a great hiding place!"

"This tree's so big. It must be hundreds of years old," said Talia.

Riki settled down on the ground and fluffed his feathers. "It's the biggest tree in the whole valley!"

"I wonder—" Talia stopped. She could hear men's voices.

"They're here!" whispered Lucas.

Riki jumped into Talia's arms and huddled against her neck. Talia held his warm, feathery body close to her, listening for any movement outside.

Lord Fortescue and his men came closer, their boots pounding on the earth. There was the cracking sound of branches breaking. Talia put her eye to a small hole in the tree trunk. She could see the soldiers now. They were hacking their way towards the circle of trees, leaving a trail of flattened plants behind them.

"This must be the place," yelled Lord Fortescue. "It was hidden from view and there's a nasty feel of magic in the air. Now, find me the firebirds and that cave of treasure!"

"Yes, sir!" The soldiers ran about the clearing, tearing down bushes and throwing stones into the treetops.

Talia held her breath, horribly afraid that a stray stone might hurt one of the firebirds.

But the men hit nothing and seemed to quickly give up throwing things. They moved on after a few minutes and the sound of crashing and banging came from further up the valley.

Lucas leaned against the inside of the tree trunk. "I hope they don't stay here long. I suppose we could sneak home now they've gone past."

Talia shook her head. "I can't go until I know the firebirds are all right."

Bangs and thumps echoed round the valley. The mountain began to rumble as if complaining about being disturbed. The sound rolled round the place like thunder. The ground shook and there were shouts from the soldiers. Talia and Lucas waited calmly. Everyone living in the Hundred Valleys knew that these mountains sometimes rumbled. It was nothing to be scared of!

The minutes passed slowly and the soldiers' thumping sounds continued. The mountain growled again. Then a column of white smoke burst into the sky. Talia was sure it came from the direction of the dragon's cave.

The shouting of the men grew louder. Footsteps pounded down the valley. Talia put her eye to the hole in the trunk and saw the soldiers run past, followed by a breathless Lord Fortescue.

"My lord, we have to get back to the boat," one of the soldiers called. "This valley isn't safe."

"What do you think I'm doing?" Lord Fortescue mopped his forehead. "This dratted place! How am I supposed to tell Lord Fitzroy that I didn't catch a single firebird? We didn't find any treasure in that cave either."

Talia beamed. She was so happy that the firebirds hadn't been found!

Lucas nudged her with his elbow and grinned.

"At least we blocked some of the magic, sir," the soldier called back.

Hurrying after his men, Lord Fortescue tripped over a trailing vine and fell over. Muttering about dirty rainforests and horrible creatures, he picked himself up and stumbled out of sight.

"Let's go to the river and watch them leave!" Lucas squeezed out of the hollow tree trunk.

"I'm right behind you." Talia edged through the hole, still holding on to Riki.

Getting through the rainforest was easy this time as the soldiers had left a wide trail of flattened undergrowth. Lucas and Talia hid in a clump of reeds and watched the soldiers rowing across the river. They worked their oars a little faster every time the mountain rumbled.

Talia sighed with relief when the men reached the other side and trudged away into the forest. "I'm so glad they've gone! I thought it might be harder to get rid of them. What a horrid, selfish man that Lord Fortescue is!"

Chapter Seven
The Disappearing Fire

Lucas turned to Talia, smiling. "So we warned the firebirds just in time."

"We did!" agreed Talia. "Let's go back and tell them that everything's all right."

Riki fluttered to the ground. "I'm so tired! Can't we rest for a bit?"

Talia crouched beside him. "Of course we can! Are you all right, Riki?"

"So tired!" Riki flopped on the ground and put his head under his wing. Talia exchanged looks with Lucas.

"That doesn't seem like him," said Lucas. "He's usually so bouncy."

Talia bit her lip. "Why don't I carry you, Riki?" The firebird didn't answer, only buried his head further under his wing. She gently picked him up. "Poor thing! It must be all the flying he's done."

As they walked back to the circle of trees, Talia held Riki close. He felt colder than before and there was no flicker of tiny flames among his feathers. The trees rustled as other firebirds emerged from their hiding places.

"Don't worry!" Talia called to them. "The soldiers have gone and the danger's over."

The firebirds nodded their heads quietly. They seemed tired too.

When the children reached the clearing, Amber-wing flew awkwardly to the ground. Her feathers looked dull and yellow. "Dear Talia," she croaked. "I'm afraid something terrible has happened."

"But Lord Fortescue has gone!" cried Talia. "Everything's going to be all right now."

"They all look so different," said Lucas. "Is it because they were scared?"

Talia put Riki down carefully. An awful worried feeling grew inside her. "It's like the fire's gone out of them," she muttered to herself. "But why would they change like that?" A sudden thought made her swing round and run up the valley.

"Where are you going?" called Lucas.

Talia kept running. Her breath caught in her throat. Where was the entrance to the cave? She knew it must be close. Maybe through these trees . . . She stopped so suddenly that Lucas, who'd run after her, nearly fell over.

Huge rocks filled the tunnel opening that led to the Cave of Wonders. They were piled one on top of the other, with smaller stones pushed in between. The cave entrance was completely blocked by the boulders.

Talia's face flushed with anger. "This must have been Lord Fortescue's men!"

"Remember how they said they'd blocked some of the magic?" said Lucas. "I bet that's what they meant."

"They didn't know how important this cave is to the firebirds and if they'd known they still wouldn't have cared!" Talia felt tears prick her eyes as she thought of Riki and how tired and ill he looked. "That's why the firebirds aren't well. They need the magic of the fire pool to keep them alive!"

Dashing forwards, she tugged at the boulders. A few smaller stones toppled from their place but the bigger rocks didn't move.

"I'll help you!" Lucas pulled at the boulders too.

"Try this one!" Talia heaved at a large rock in the middle. Lucas joined her, taking the other side of the boulder. They pulled and pulled. Talia's fingers ached from gripping on to the jagged stone.

"It's stuck!" she said at last. "It's not moving at all."

Lucas aimed an angry kick at the boulder. "Stupid rocks! No wonder we heard all that

banging and crashing when the soldiers were
here. They were building a wall of rocks all that
time."

"Careful!" gasped Talia. "What if the rocks
tumble backwards and roll down the slope into
the fire pool? It could destroy the pool forever!"

A group of firebirds had gathered behind the
children. Riki and Amber-Wing were among
them.

"We cannot survive without the Cave of Wonders," said Amber-wing sadly. "Already many of us can no longer fly and it has only been a few hours since we bathed in the fire pool."

"There has to be a way to open the cave again." Talia glared at the rocks.

"If we could find some strong sticks, maybe we could lever the rocks out," suggested Lucas. "Or we could run back to Kura and get people from the village to come and help us."

"It'd take too long to get home and explain everything." Talia frowned. "The firebirds need help *now*!"

"Then we need someone bigger and stronger than we are." Lucas folded his arms. "We'll never manage this on our own."

"There's no one here that's bigger than us!" cried Talia. "We have to think of something else."

"I'm trying to think!" snapped Lucas. "You're

not coming up with many ideas."

"Arguing isn't going to help us!" said Talia, pushing her hair over her shoulder. "Wait a minute! You're completely right! We need someone bigger and stronger. Someone MUCH bigger and stronger!"

Lucas frowned. "Huh? What do you mean?"

"There's one creature in this valley that has to be stronger than either of us," said Talia. "The red-back dragon!"

"Do you think that's a good idea?" Lucas said doubtfully. "What if it doesn't like humans? What if it breathes fire at us? That smoke coming from its cave looks pretty deadly."

"I'm going to try talking to him," said Talia, with a determined look. "It's the best hope we've got."

Chapter Eight
The Dragon's Cave

Talia knelt beside Riki and stroked his dull yellow feathers. "We're going to get help," she told him. "We won't be long." She looked round at the other firebirds, each one slumped on the ground.

Riki lifted one limp wing. "Come back soon, Talia."

Talia swallowed. She hated leaving him but she had to get help.

"I think the cave is this way," said Lucas. "I remember seeing that white smoke when we'd

just crossed the river."

Talia and Lucas fought their way through
the rainforest, looking for the entrance to the
dragon's cave. At last they found the deep chasm
in a gap between the trees.

"I still don't know if this is a good idea," said
Lucas, staring into the hole.

Talia crouched down by the edge, her
stomach twisting. "Excuse me!" she called into
the hole. "Sorry to disturb you but we really
need your help."

There was no sound from inside.

"My name's Talia and this is Lucas!" Talia
tried again. "The firebirds are in trouble and
that's why we need you."

She waited. There was still no sound.

Talia lay down and peered into the chasm.
The jagged rock scratched her arms. Way down,
she could see a red and black shape sprawled
across the cave floor. One bright-green eye
glinted in the darkness. Then it snapped shut.

Scrambling up, Talia looked around for something that would work as a rope. There were plenty of trailing vines in the trees. "Can you get that long vine for me?" she asked Lucas. "I'm going inside."

"You're going down into its lair? You're crazy!" Lucas shinned up the Izzala tree and pulled down the vine.

"The dragon heard me. I'm sure of it," said Talia. "If I get closer he won't be able to ignore me."

Lucas tied the vine to the bottom of the tree trunk. "Maybe being ignored by a dragon is a good thing!" He tugged on the vine to check it would hold, before throwing it into the hole.

Using the vine like a rope, Talia climbed into the dark cave. Her feet slipped a little halfway down but she held tight and recovered her foothold. At the bottom she spun round to see if the dragon had noticed her, but his eyes were firmly shut.

 76

Water dripped from the damp, grey walls and the cool air made Talia shiver. The sleeping dragon almost filled the whole cave and Talia had to step carefully round him. The creature's black wings were folded and his tail curled around his body. Large red spines jutted from his back. His stomach rose and fell as he breathed slowly.

Talia wondered if he really was fast asleep. She remembered that bright-green eye glinting. She tiptoed as close to his head as she dared. His black nostrils twitched.

Talia leaned closer. "Are you really asleep?"

A faint rumble began at the back of the dragon's throat. Talia pressed herself against the cave wall, her heart pounding.

The dragon's jaws parted. "Yes!" he hissed. Then he was silent again. He hadn't even opened his eyes.

The vine shook and Lucas landed on the cave floor. "You looked like you needed help," he whispered to Talia.

"We've got to wake this dragon." Talia leaned forwards again, saying loudly, "Hello! I'm sorry to wake you! My name is Talia."

Nothing happened.

"Hello!" yelled Lucas. "We come in peace!"

"Wake up!" shouted Talia.

The dragon didn't even twitch.

They shouted again and again. Then they tapped his front legs (keeping well away from his huge jaws). They even tried tickling him.

"It's hard to know whether a dragon would actually feel a tickle," said Talia at last. "They have such tough hide." Glancing at the dragon's mouth, she wondered if she'd seen the twitch of a smile.

"We're running out of time," said Lucas. "The firebirds will be getting weaker."

"There must be something else we can try!" said Talia desperately. "What do red-back dragons eat?"

The dragon opened one green eye. "Izzala flowers," he rumbled, his booming voice echoed round the cave.

Talia jumped. "I *knew* he could hear us," she whispered to Lucas. "He said he eats Izzala flowers. Quick, climb back up and get some."

Lucas shinned up the vine and started throwing Izzala flowers into the cave. Their honey-sweet scent filled the air. Talia gathered a large bunch of the flowers and held them close to the dragon's nostrils. "Would you like these? I just need to talk to you about the firebirds. They're in terrible trouble."

The dragon slowly opened his eyes and yawned. "I'm not really hungry after all."

"But you *have* to help us!" cried Talia,

forgetting to speak carefully. "This is an emergency. The firebirds are ill!"

The dragon's eyes narrowed and the end of his tail whipped to and fro. "I *have* to? I am not accustomed to being told what to do." He coughed, and white smoke streamed from his mouth. Then he closed his eyes again and settled his chin on the ground.

Talia had leapt back to avoid the smoke. "Sorry! I didn't mean to be rude but we're running out of time."

"How is it that you can speak to me?" the dragon asked, his eyes still closed.

Talia had forgotten that she hadn't explained about her Speaking Stone. She took the little rock from around her neck and opened it to reveal the hollow inside. The crystals gleamed, casting flecks of golden light across the dark cave walls.

The dragon peeked through one eye. Then both his eyes snapped open and he lifted his head. "THAT is very shiny!" The words rumbled in his throat. "Come closer and let me see!"

Talia edged a little closer. She explained that the stone let her talk to magical animals. Then she quickly told him about the soldiers who had come to Jalmar Valley and how they'd blocked the doorway to the Cave of Wonders.

The dragon listened but his green eyes kept straying back to the little hollow stone. "Silly people!" he snorted at the end. "I thought I'd heard a lot of noise and bother."

"So the firebirds really need you! They can't survive without the magic of the fire pool," explained Talia. "Lucas and I couldn't move the boulders but I'm sure you're so strong that you could do it easily." She waited, hoping desperately that he wouldn't go back to sleep again.

The dragon studied her, his black tail swishing. Lucas climbed down the vine. He and Talia waited for the dragon's decision.

At last the dragon heaved himself up. From under his belly rolled a handful of shiny rocks and pebbles. "I will help you on one condition," he growled. "You must give me your sparkling stone."

"You want to keep my stone?" said Talia.

The dragon gazed down. "Yes. If you want my help you must give it to me now."

Talia felt like there was something heavy inside her chest. Even though she'd only worn it for a few days, she loved her magical stone. But the firebirds needed the dragon's help. She held out the dangling stone and it glittered in the darkness.

"Talia, don't!" cried Lucas. "You won't be able to talk to the firebirds any more. They won't understand you."

"I know." Talia let the dragon take the thread in his jaws. "But this is the only way to move those rocks. I can't let Riki down."

Chapter Nine
A Surprising New Friend

The red-back dragon carefully dropped the magical stone among his other shiny pebbles. Growling, he opened one black wing and tilted it to the ground.

"Does he want us to climb on his back?" said Lucas, his eyes round.

"I suppose so. I can't understand him now that I don't have my stone." Talia started climbing the dragon's wing. It felt tough and surprisingly springy beneath her feet.

"Wait! What if he doesn't really want us to get

on?" said Lucas. "What if he gets angry?"

"Then I guess he'll find a way of telling us."
Talia clambered over the red spines and sat
down on the dragon's back. "Don't you want
to tell everyone in Kura that you rode on a
dragon?"

"They'd never believe me!" Lucas scrambled
up the wing to join her.

The dragon growled again and launched
himself into the open. Talia blinked, dazzled
by the sunlight after the dark of the cave. Each
beat of the dragon's wings took them higher,
until they were gliding over the forest. Talia
gazed down at the beautiful valley and the
mist swirling gently over the Izzala trees. Air
whooshed past her face and she held on tight.

After only a minute, the dragon dipped back
into the trees. Firebirds scattered as he landed
heavily beside the Cave of Wonders. The birds'
bright feathers had turned to dull yellow.

Talia and Lucas slid off the dragon's back.

Talia gazed at Riki lying weakly on the ground. She longed to pick him up and cuddle him but there was no time to lose. Running to the pile of rocks, she waved to the dragon to follow.

The red-back dragon sniffed the boulders blocking the mouth of the cave and gave a deep growl that made Talia shiver. He gripped a rock with his great black claws and launched into the air. Talia scrambled back to avoid his beating wings.

When the rock didn't move, the dragon tried again. Puffing out his cheeks he heaved at the boulder, leaving long scrape marks across the stone. The rock didn't move. The dragon let out a great roar that echoed round the valley.

"This isn't working," said Lucas. "The soldiers jammed the rocks in too well."

Talia ran to the cave entrance, waving to the dragon to stop. "Lucas, help me!" She began pulling the smaller stones from between the boulders. "If we move these little ones he'll be

able to get a better grip on the large rocks."

Lucas and Talia worked quickly, pulling out as many of the smaller rocks as they could. A soft growl rumbled at the back of the dragon's throat.

"That's probably enough!" Lucas grabbed Talia's arm and they stood back.

The dragon grasped the biggest rock and pulled. There was a long grinding sound and the rock came loose. The dragon tossed it aside and seized another one. That too came free, so he grabbed another and another.

As soon as the dragon stopped to rest, Talia and Lucas dived forwards, moving all the smaller rocks and piling them out of the way. A wave of heat blew through the gaps in the wall, making Talia's skin tingle. The firebirds lifted their heads as they felt the warm breeze. They squawked gently to each other.

As the dragon moved more of the boulders, a cascade of smaller rocks came loose and trickled down the slope. The creature gave a triumphant roar. Whirling round, he knocked the last of the boulders away with a great swing of his spiky tail.

"Thank you!" Talia bowed deeply to the dragon.

The dragon nodded to the children before lumbering away to eat some flowers from a nearby Izzala tree.

Lucas moved the last few rocks out of the cave entrance and dusted off his hands. Amber-wing called to the other firebirds and they tottered towards the cave, their frail wings lifted in hope.

Talia saw Riki struggling to his feet. Dashing over, she scooped him up and gently set him down by the mouth of the cave. He gave a delighted squawk and stumbled into the tunnel with the other firebirds.

Talia sank on to a boulder, suddenly overwhelmed by tiredness. "I'm so glad they can reach their fire pool again."

"It was a great idea to ask the dragon for help," Lucas told her. "And I don't think Lord Fortescue and his men will be back. They seemed pretty scared by the noises from the mountains."

Talia nodded, watching the last firebirds

crowd into the cave entrance. "They wanted to find gold but they missed the real treasure that's already here – the animals!"

Suddenly there was an excited squeak and a flash of golden wings, as Riki flew out of the dark tunnel. His feathers sparkled as he swooped down to Talia's knee. He chattered into her ear, pecked her gently on the cheek and then nestled on to her lap.

"You look beautiful!" cried Talia. "I'm so happy you're well again." Her heart ached as she saw a look of confusion spread across the firebird's face. She pointed to her neck where she'd always hung the magical stone. "I can't understand you any more because I don't have the Speaking Stone. But it doesn't matter! You look amazing, Riki!"

Riki squawked back to her, throwing his bright wings around her neck.

The red-back dragon watched them as he chewed Izzala flowers. His bright-green eyes

narrowed as Riki and Talia hugged each other.
He gave a snort, spread his great wings and flew
off into the distance.

More and more firebirds poured out of the
Cave of Wonders. Their feathers gleamed like
sunlight and the crests on their heads stood
bright and tall. They chattered to each other,
swooping into the air on their sparkling wings.

Lucas grinned. "They're such awesome
creatures!"

"Yes they are!" Talia smiled. "I think they're celebrating."

All the firebirds had taken to the sky. Gliding back and forth, the flock made a criss-cross pattern. Their graceful flight looked like dancing in the air. The sun began to set and the shadows of the trees grew longer, but the firebirds' dance went on.

"That's strange!" Lucas twisted round. "What's he come back for?"

Talia turned to look. The dragon swooped through the darkening sky, circling the hillside before landing heavily beside them. He loomed over Talia. His bright-green eyes looked straight into hers.

"What is it?" said Talia, her heart racing.

A deep growl sounded in the dragon's throat. Talia noticed something dangling from his mouth. It flashed in fiery colours as it caught the light. Bending down, the dragon dropped the Speaking Stone into Talia's lap.

She clasped it tightly. "Oh! But I thought you wanted it as payment for your help."

"You deserve to keep it. I see that now!" growled the dragon. "That is no ordinary stone and you are no ordinary girl! You are a friend to magical animals and now you can speak to us as much as you wish."

"Thank you so much!" gasped Talia. "Please tell me your name."

"I am Bellegar, the only red-back dragon in the hidden valley." The dragon bowed to Talia and Lucas solemnly. "And I am very pleased to have met you both."

Talia returned the dragon's bow before showing Lucas her stone. "His name is Bellegar. He just told me. Hasn't today been amazing?"

"Amazing but very strange!" said Lucas, bowing to Bellegar. "No one back in the village is going to believe that we made friends with a dragon!"

Chapter Ten
A Present for Lucas

The sun set behind the trees. As the sky darkened, the firebirds' magical feathers shone in a blaze of orange and gold. They carried on dancing in the air. Now and then a firebird soared straight upwards, its wings shimmering like a firework.

Bellegar told Talia of how he came to live in the hidden valley when he was a very young dragon and how he liked the peace and quiet. Talia promised to make him a special bowl when she returned home and to paint it with

pictures of the red flowers he loved so much.

Just as Talia was growing tired, the wind blew
harder and the trees swayed. A dark shape came
flying over the river and circled overhead. The
firebirds called to each other in surprise.

"What is it? What's happening?" asked Talia
in alarm.

"It's another dragon," Bellegar told her. "A
storm dragon!"

The wind swirled as the huge creature set
down on the rocky slope, making the ground
tremble. "Greetings, brother!" he rumbled. "I
haven't met a red-back dragon for many years.
Greetings to you too, young firebirds. My name
is Windrunner."

"I'm Bellegar," replied the red-back dragon.

A girl with blonde plaits slid down from the
storm dragon's back. She was wearing a black
dress and a white apron.

"Sophy!" cried Talia. "I should have known it
was you!"

"Hello again!" Sophy hugged Talia. "I'm so sorry I couldn't come straightaway when you needed me. I've been so worried ever since I got your message!"

"But everything's all right now!" said Talia.
"Lucas, this is Sophy, who works as a maid at
the royal castle. She's the one I told you about –
the girl who gave me the Speaking Stone."

Lucas grinned. "Do you always fly around on
a dragon?"

"Only when I can get away from Lord
Fitzroy," said Sophy with a groan. "He's the
knight that hates magical animals and he's
persuaded the queen that they're dangerous too.
He's the reason I was trapped at the castle. But
tell me about your adventure!"

Talia explained how the soldiers had arrived
looking for the hidden valley. Lucas interrupted
now and then to add things to the tale. Sophy's
eyes widened as she heard the part about the fire
pool.

"So I was lucky that Lucas and Bellegar
were here too," finished Talia. "We all worked
together to unblock the cave and now the
firebirds are well again."

"Brilliant!" Sophy beamed. "You've done really well with your Speaking Stone." She fumbled in her apron pocket and brought out a small bag made of purple velvet.

"Is that where you keep the stones?" asked Lucas.

Sophy nodded. "I found them among a pile of things the queen was throwing away and I've kept them ever since." She opened the bag and showed Lucas the little grey rocks. "You wouldn't know just from looking at them that they have such amazing magic inside."

Talia looked from Sophy to Lucas. She thought she knew what Sophy was about to do.

"Lucas," Sophy began solemnly. "Having a Speaking Stone is a big responsibility and you have to love magical animals. Would you like to try the stones and see if there's one for you?"

Lucas's mouth dropped open.

"You'd be great with a Speaking Stone. I know you would!" said Talia.

"I'd like to try," said Lucas.

"Then hold out your hands and let's see what happens." Sophy dropped the stones into Lucas's hands one by one. The sixth one started to glow.

"It's getting hot!" gasped Lucas. "Is that meant to happen?"

"Yes!" said Talia. "Just wait – it gets even better!"

They held their breath. The magical stone glowed brighter and brighter, until suddenly it broke open. Inside was a tiny cave of shiny green crystals.

"Awesome!" breathed Lucas.

"Remember, it *has* to stay a secret," Sophy told him. "So wear it under your shirt and don't tell anyone."

"I won't! I'm going to see if it works right now!" Lucas dashed over to the dragons and started talking to them.

Talia smiled at Sophy. "I think he'll make a great friend to magical animals."

"I think so too!" Sophy smiled back. "I'm so glad I finally got away from the castle to find you all."

"Was it really tricky?" asked Talia.

"Awful!" Sophy sighed. "Sir Fitzroy had guards watching the gate all day so I waited till Windrunner flew past the castle tower after dark. I slipped straight out of the window on to his back!"

"That's so exciting!" said Talia. "But why is Sir Fitzroy acting like that?"

Sophy's brow wrinkled. "He's been suspicious

ever since Ava and I rescued the sky unicorn. He didn't see that it was me, but he knows *someone* is helping the magical animals. And then he found some information about Speaking Stones in one of the castle books, so now he's on the lookout for them."

"It would be terrible if he found them!" cried Talia.

"It would ruin everything!" Sophy put all the stones back into the velvet bag and gave it to Talia. "That's why I want you to keep these for a while. Sir Fitzroy could order me to turn out my pockets and discover the whole bag! They'll be safer with you."

Talia took the bag, her heart racing. "Are you sure?"

Sophy smiled. "Of course I am! You could ask Bellegar to carry you on his back. Find new people who love magical animals and pass on more of the Speaking Stones."

"I will!" Talia held the bag tightly to her chest.

"Thanks, Sophy!"

"Bye, Talia! Bye, Lucas!" Sophy climbed on to Windrunner's back. "I'll try to come and see you again soon!"

"Goodbye! Thanks for my magical stone," called Lucas.

Talia waved as Sophy and Windrunner flew into the night sky. She had been trusted with all the magical stones. She wouldn't let Sophy down!

"Talia!" Riki flew into her arms. "Will there be more adventures?"

Talia smiled. "Yes, there'll be lots more adventures!" She hugged Riki, feeling his warm feathers against her cheek. Together they watched the other firebirds swooping and soaring through the air, their golden wings glittering in the starlit sky.

Enjoy more
amazing animal adventures
at Zoe's Rescue Zoo!